Oscar's
Starry Night

Look out for
Oscar Needs A Friend

Scholastic Children's Books,
Commonwealth House, 1-19 New Oxford Street,
London WC1A 1NU, UK
London ~ New York ~ Toronto ~ Sydney ~ Auckland
Mexico City ~ New Delhi ~ Hong Kong

Published by Scholastic Ltd, 1999

Text copyright © Joan Stimson, 1999
Illustrations copyright © Meg Rutherford, 1999

ISBN 0 590 11421 2

Printed in China

Oscar's Starry Night

by Joan Stimson

illustrated by Meg Rutherford

SCHOLASTIC
PRESS

Oscar was a bear who was often over-excited.

He whooped when he whizzed down his slide.

He shrieked when he took Mum by surprise.

And if ever he tried anything new or adventurous, Oscar couldn't wait to begin.

One morning, Oscar woke up feeling more excited than he'd ever felt before.

That afternoon, he was going to play with Ollie. And that night, he was going to sleep at Ollie's house.

When it was time to leave, Oscar ran on ahead.
"Look! Ollie's coming to meet me," he cried.
And he waved goodbye to Mum.

All afternoon, the two bears raced and chased each other.

Oscar kept shouting across the mountainside.
"I'm going to sleep at Ollie's house!"

And when Ollie told him they were going to sleep outside, Oscar was even more excited.

After supper, the two bears made up their beds.

"It's going to be a fine, warm night," said Ollie's mum. "And I'll be just inside if you need me."

Oscar snuggled down eagerly. This was the moment he'd been waiting for.
"Isn't it brilliant out here?" said Ollie.

But by now, night was falling. Everything
looked different in the dark. And Oscar began
to feel anxious.

"WHOOOH! WHOOOH!"
An owl flew by.
And made him jump.

Strange shadows in the gloom made him shiver.

Then, worst of all, Oscar felt something soft and fluttery on his face.

"What's that?" he squeaked in a panic.
"It's only me trying to find your tickle spot,"
giggled Ollie.

But by now, Oscar was feeling
silly as well as nervous.
"What if Ollie doesn't want to
be my friend any more?" he
wondered miserably.

"Isn't it brilliant out here?" said Ollie for the tenth time. Oscar was too upset to answer.

But suddenly Ollie bounced across from his bed and onto Oscar's.

"And the most brilliant thing of all," he cried,

"is that you're here. Because, otherwise,"
Ollie told Oscar, "I'd be . . . scared!"

Oscar sat up in amazement.
"I was a bit scared myself at first," he admitted.
"But I'm all right now!"

Just at that moment, Ollie's mum bustled outside.
"Now, who's ready for a drink," she said,
"after all that talking?"
Oscar and Ollie both
wanted a drink.

Then they wanted to see
the waterfall by moonlight.

At last the two bears settled down.
"See how many stars you can count,"
said Ollie's mum, "before you
fall asleep."

"Oooh!" cried Oscar and Ollie, as they turned on their backs. And gazed upwards.

"Oooh!" they cried again,
as a shooting star dived
across the sky.

"Isn't it brilliant out here?" said Ollie when
his mum went inside.

This time, Oscar nodded happily.
"It's all brilliant," he told Ollie. "And one day
soon I'd like to sleep at your house . . . again!"